Teen Issues

SELF-HARM

Cath Senker

Heinemann LIBRARY

Chicago, Illinois

www.capstonepub.com
Visit our website to find out more information about Heinemann-Raintree books.

To order:

☎ Phone 800-747-4992

💻 Visit www.capstonepub.com to browse our catalog and order online.

Edited by Andrew Farrow, Adam Miller, and Vaarunika Dharmapala
Designed by Steve Mead and Clare Webber

Originated by Capstone Global Library Ltd
Printed and bound in China by Leo Paper Products Ltd

16 15 14 13 12
10 9 8 7 6 5 4 3 2 1

Library of Congress Cataloging-in-Publication Data

Senker, Cath.

Self-harm / Cath Senker.—1st ed.

p. cm.—(Teen issues)

Includes bibliographical references and index.

ISBN 978-1-4329-6537-2 (hb)—ISBN 978-1-4329-6542-6 (pb) 1. Self-mutilation. I. Title.

RC552.S4S46 2013

616.85'82—dc23   2011039241

Acknowledgments

We would like to thank the following for permission to reproduce photographs: Alamy pp. 15 (© Travelfile), 23 (© Design Pics Inc.), 24, 38 (© Janine Wiedel Photolibrary), 32 (© Keith Dannemiller), 42 (© Avatra Images), 49 (© Frances Roberts); Corbis pp. 4 (© Ephraim Ben-Shimon), 9 (© Radius Images), 10 (© Christina Richards), 16 (© Simon Marcus), 28 (© SW Productions/Design Pics), 34 (© Ocean); Getty Images p. 6 (Image Source), 12 (New York Daily News), 30 (Christopher Furlong); Shutterstock pp. 20 (© Anthony Bolan), 26 (© Edw), 37 (© Elena Elisseeva), 40 (© Christopher Edwin Nuzzaco), 45 (© Anton Albert), 47 (© Christopher Edwin Nuzzaco); Superstock p. 19 (© age fotostock).

Cover photograph of a girl hiding her head in her hands reproduced with permission of Getty Images (Peter Dazeley/Photographer's Choice).

The author would like to thank Shelley Holland, youth counselor (www.counseling4brighton.co.uk), for her invaluable help in writing this book.

The author would also like to acknowledge the following sources for real-life stories: pp. 4–5, Holly's story: TheSite.org; pp. 14–15, Stuart's story: TheSite.org; p. 23, Lila's story: Get Connected; p. 38–39, Samira's story: TheSite.org; p. 47, Hannah's story: Young Minds.

In order to protect the privacy of individuals featured in this book, some names may have been changed.

Every effort has been made to contact copyright holders of any material reproduced in this book. Any omissions will be rectified in subsequent printings if notice is given to the publisher.

Disclaimer

All the Internet addresses (URLs) given in this book were valid at the time of going to press. However, due to the dynamic nature of the Internet, some addresses may have changed, or sites may have changed or ceased to exist since publication. While the author and publisher regret any inconvenience this may cause readers, no responsibility for any such changes can be accepted by either the author or the publisher.

CONTENTS

Some words are shown in bold, **like this**. You can find out what they mean by looking in the glossary.

SELF-HARM

If young people are depressed and feel that no one understands, the situation could lead them to self-harm.

HOLLY'S STORY:
CUTTING GOT ME THROUGH THE DARK DAYS

"Self-harming by burning and cutting was helpful for a certain period of my life. It got me through the dark days.

I began self-harming when I was 13, after my parents split up. I was feeling really upset and depressed. One day, I noticed the scissors on the coffee table. I used them to cut myself. Cutting gave me a '**euphoric** release' [from the **depression**] and I began to do it regularly. I almost looked forward to going home to do it. For me, it was a coping mechanism to get through each day, rather than to punish myself.

After the initial reason for self-harming, I found I used it when other difficulties arose, such as arguments or money worries. But it got to the point where I knew it was wrong. Other people's reactions finally made me realize that I had to stop—I didn't feel that self-harming was hurting me, but it was damaging other people. Sometimes, a friend would find me on the floor bleeding and screaming in pain and would help to bandage my arm, in tears herself.

I gradually stopped self-harming after several years of doing it every couple of days. Even though I was still feeling low, I discovered other ways to deal with my problems, and I guess I was feeling more comfortable with myself. I found that **distraction** always stopped me from self-harming, whether it was watching television, taking a bath, or going for a walk.

Now, six months later, I'm not sure that I will never hurt myself again, but for the time being I have definitely stopped self-harming."

Holly's story about what caused her to self-harm and how she stopped is not unusual. Read on to find out more about what drives people to do it, the emotions involved, and the facts that explode common myths about self-harm.

WHY DO SOME PEOPLE SELF-HARM?

A young person who is finding it difficult to express negative emotions may turn to self-harm as an outlet.

So, what is self-harm? We need some facts to understand it. There is a wide spectrum of **self-destructive** activities, from risky behavior and indirectly hurting oneself to deliberate self-harm. People may take unnecessary risks with their health. Some do not take care of themselves, failing to eat a healthy diet or to get enough exercise. They might **abuse** alcohol or drugs or develop an **eating disorder**. Perhaps they stay in an abusive relationship. Deliberate self-harm is when people hurt themselves on purpose.

Deliberate self-harm

Deliberate self-harm is a type of behavior that is not intended to result in **suicide**. It may be a one-time or occasional release, following an upsetting event, or it may happen regularly. People may self-harm as a way to cope with stress because they are finding it hard to tackle a difficult situation. Self-harm can take many forms. Some people intentionally cut, scratch, or burn themselves. They may even swallow poisonous objects, such as batteries.

Self-harmers find that hurting themselves can relieve stress in the short term. If people are overwhelmed by angry feelings or depression but cannot express what is upsetting them, they look for a way to feel better. Hurting themselves makes some people feel better in the short term, because it numbs the emotional pain.

Self-harm is a way to push back the feelings for a short time, providing temporary relief from the **symptoms** of the problem. Yet the underlying issue has not been resolved, so it is bound to re-emerge.

> " [Self-harm] made the pain go away . . . I wouldn't have to cry and I'd feel happy again. "
>
> *Tammy (in her early twenties)*

What causes self-harm?

Self-harm is a symptom of a deep-rooted problem in a person's life. The teenage years can be a challenging time. Young people must deal with changes in their bodies and emotions and their developing sexuality. As a result, poor body image is common. Many people feel that they do not live up to society's ideal of good looks. Teenagers often suffer from a lack of confidence in their appearance, which can make them depressed and lower their **self-esteem**.

At the same time, young people are going through an important stage of their education. Academic pressure can be an issue. The burden of schoolwork and the high expectations of teachers and parents can make learning stressful.

Isolation can make self-image problems worse. Some young people experience bullying and are not being helped by friends or responsible adults. They may lack friends or a supportive family. Indeed, the teenage years are a common time for family tensions to surface, as young people aim to become more independent. They may clash with their parents over how much freedom they should be allowed. As a result, family relationships could deteriorate, and young people may feel unable to confide in their parents.

"I started cutting myself when I could no longer cope with being bullied about my weight and the way I look."

Josephine (age 16)

Sometimes difficult life events, such as divorce or a death in the family, can **trigger** self-harm. A tragedy, especially if it is sudden or particularly shocking, such as suicide, can be a cause of self-harm. If a close friend or relative is self-harming, this can have an influence as well. However, it is often not a single issue that leads to self-harm, but rather a combination of daily stresses and strains.

Being bullied at school may contribute to feelings of isolation and stress, which can in turn lead to self-harm.

Coping strategies

It is important to remember that everyone has troubles and obstacles to face in life. The crucial question is, how do you handle them? Everyone needs coping strategies, and frequently people cannot manage alone. They need support. If some people feel they cannot deal with the challenges in life, then they might resort to self-harming.

TRUE OR FALSE?

Self-harm is a suicide attempt.

Mostly False. Self-harm is a way of dealing with painful feelings rather than a suicide attempt. However, people who self-harm may have an increased risk of trying to kill themselves in the future if their problems are not dealt with (see page 21).

Immediate triggers

Why would people want to injure themselves and cause themselves pain? People self-harm to release tensions caused by school, family, or **peer** pressure and to cope with tough circumstances. They may be experiencing strong feelings such as unhappiness, depression, fear, or despair and find physical pain more bearable than the emotional agony.

Physical pain can give people a temporary sense of control over their lives if they are in a situation they cannot manage. As one teenager, Mel, put it, "When I do it, it feels like one thing that I have control over. It's one thing that I can decide, how hard I hit that wall." It may be that the worse these people feel, the harder they hurt themselves.

Another reason might be to make their suffering show. For instance, young people who have been abused may feel that no one believes the abuse actually happened because there are no physical marks. However, they face extreme **psychological** pain. They are hurt by what happened to them and feel shame or guilt, even though the abuse was not their fault. The self-harm may be a means of self-punishment. When these people self-injure, the hurt becomes visible and makes their mental pain real, too. These people are expressing the terrible agony of their feelings.

Self-harming can give young people the illusion that they have control over what happens to them.

How does self-harm seem to help?

People who self-harm frequently say that their troubles make them feel numb or dead inside. When they undergo physical pain, they feel alive again. Somehow, they are communicating their misery, even though at the time they are not able to talk about it to anyone. When they are feeling extremely tense, self-harming relieves the pressure. Immediately after the injury, these people experience relief and a temporary release from their difficulties. Some people say that the bad feelings seem to flow away with the blood they have released.

"I used to feel emotions building up inside me—and cutting myself felt as if I was releasing the valve on a pressure cooker. The moment that I saw the blood, I experienced a tremendous sense of relief and was able to relax. It was also a reminder that I was alive."

Kirsti Reeve, who now runs a web site to support self-harmers

"I felt as if I'd been taken over by bad things inside me. The deeper you went in, the more you could get them out. That would be the release—getting it out."

Vicky (in her twenties)

Copycat self-harming

Some people self-harm because they think it is a cool thing to do. They may copy celebrities who do it. Singer Marilyn Manson became well known for self-harming. He had endured a **traumatic** childhood, with a father who had a mental-health condition. Manson suffered from low self-esteem. He used to cut himself on stage, as he said, "to show people my pain." Unfortunately, some of his fans chose to self-injure to imitate him.

Celebrity self-harmers

Other celebrities who have admitted to self-harm include singer and actress Demi Lovato and actress Christina Ricci. Ricci used to burn her hands and arms with cigarettes and later explained why, saying: "You know how your brain shuts down from pain? The pain would be so bad, it would force my body to slow down, and I wouldn't be as anxious. It made me calm." Once she displayed her scarred hand in an interview. Singer Amy Winehouse was also photographed with scars and scratches on her arms. However, unlike Manson, these stars self-harmed privately, not for an audience.

Self-harm in religion

Images of self-harm can be found in various religious traditions. For example, Christianity includes the belief that Christ suffered for the sins of the world. Pain is seen to cleanse people from sin. Among Shia Muslims, the festival of Ashura commemorates the death of Hussein, the grandson of the Prophet Muhammad. A few Shias whip themselves with chains or cut themselves with razors to remember the suffering of Hussein, although most other Shia Muslims discourage this custom.

Actress Christina Ricci has spoken openly about her self-harming.

Peer pressure

Celebrities have been blamed for encouraging self-harm, but certain influences closer to home may also have an effect. If someone in a **clique** self-harms, others may follow suit, and it can become a feature of the group's behavior. If people do it once and get a buzz out of it, they may repeat the action, and it becomes a habit.

Self-harm online: The debate

Some people put videos of self-harm techniques on web sites such as YouTube. Experts do not believe that such videos will lead an otherwise happy person to start self-harming, but they may encourage those who already self-harm to continue to do so. It offers them an online community of support, which makes self-injury appear like a normal activity. Viewers can also find guidance on different ways to injure themselves. On the other hand, many people use forums to gain **empathy** and support to stop self-harming, so self-harm sites do not necessarily promote self-harm.

Despite the great visibility of self-harm online, regular self-harm in a young person usually indicates underlying dilemmas rather than copycat behavior. It is generally people's own experiences, not those of others, that lead them to hurt themselves.

THINK ABOUT THIS

Do television soap operas with storylines about self-harm encourage the practice?

In Canada, the storyline in *Degrassi: The Next Generation* has included self-injury. For instance, in the "Whisper to a Scream" episode, Ellie's dad goes off to the army and her mom turns to alcohol. With no one to help her to handle the stress of her hectic life, Ellie starts cutting herself. Some people argue that by showing self-harm and the context in which it can occur, such programs open up debate about the subject. Others are concerned that showing self-injury on popular programs could encourage viewers to try it themselves.

STUART'S STORY: A BAD EXPERIENCE LED ME TO SELF-HARM

"I was 19 when I started self-harming. I was working at a camp, where a close friend was violently attacked. I was deeply upset by this. When I came home, I fell into a bout of severe depression. I felt really lost and didn't know what to do with myself. One day I lashed out and smashed a mirror, cutting myself. The pain really helped me to focus and cleared my head. From then on, self-harm became my way of coping.

I was OK during the day and could distract myself. But the evenings were difficult. Whenever I had time to myself, that's when my demons returned. I felt **vulnerable** and fell into self-harming.

Then I went to college and soon became involved in a relationship. My girlfriend was awesome. She stood by me, but didn't judge me; she offered help if I wanted it. She encouraged me to go to my doctor to ask for help. But the doctor was unsympathetic. She couldn't understand why an intelligent person like me was self-harming. It turned me off from the idea of seeing professionals. I began to hate myself and continued to self-harm. This was how I took care of myself; the self-harm stopped me from doing something worse.

Later, I went to another doctor who allowed me the freedom to talk about my problem. This was good because it had been tough for my girlfriend being my only source of support. I still felt depressed, though—until out of the blue a wild idea changed my life.

A friend suggested that I take a bike trip across Asia with him. I flew to the Philippines, trained, and began the bike trip. Cycling was intensely rewarding—being physically active helped me cope with my worries. Exhausted after climbing a steep hill, I felt the high I used to get from self-harm. After the trip, I returned home and continued to exercise. I bought a punching bag, which was helpful for releasing feelings. I could let out all my frustrations and anger on that bag and improve my fitness at the same time! Now I know that if I feel well physically, I will feel good mentally, too."

Many forms of physical exercise can help people to cope with difficult feelings.

Why does self-harming calm people down?

Studies have shown that when people are emotionally overwhelmed, self-harm brings the tension back to a bearable level. So, if people have strong and uncomfortable emotions they cannot deal with, they know that feeling pain will reduce this feeling very quickly. They may still feel bad, but they no longer feel panic.

WHO SELF-HARMS?

At home, families can often be involved in their own individual activities rather than spending time together. Sometimes it is easy to feel lonely even in a group.

Self-harm occurs around the world. People of different ages, both men and women, may self-harm. Yet self-injury seems more common in young people and those who have complicated life problems. Painful episodes in early life may lead people to self-harm later on.

Girls or boys?

It appears that more girls and young women self-harm than boys or men. An organization called the Samaritans has indicated that girls are four times more likely to self-harm than boys. This might be because **sexual abuse** is one of the triggers for self-harm, and more females have suffered this than males. Yet it may simply be that fewer boys and men admit to self-harm in surveys. Also, young men are more likely to hit themselves or break their own bones as a form of self-harm, but it can look like they have had an accident or been in a fight.

Young or old?

It appears that the majority of people who self-harm are young—between the ages of 11 and 25. The average age when people start self-harming is 12. Young people encounter pressure from school and peers and may find it hard to sort out their troubles. It may be difficult to confide in friends and family. Today, families tend to spend less time together—people watch television, use the computer, or listen to music on their own rather than taking part in activities as a family. If someone is upset, he or she may be left to deal with the situation alone.

If the parents have difficulties, their children are more likely to develop problems. As the self-harm prevention organization Zest describes it, generally "a hurt individual is part of a hurt family."

TRUE OR FALSE?

People who self-harm are "crazy"

False. People who self-harm do not necessarily have a mental illness. They are simply experiencing severe emotional stress.

People with challenges

Those experiencing challenging life situations can be prone to self-harming as a coping strategy. People in the lowest social classes are at a disadvantage in society. They are likely to work in low-paid jobs and be short on money or to be affected by unemployment or homelessness. People who are socially isolated may be at risk, too. This means people who are living alone, divorced, or single parents. Those who endure **discrimination** because of their race, religion, skin color, or lifestyle may also have a higher tendency to self-harm.

Young people in residential settings—for example, in the army, prison, or at boarding school—may be vulnerable because they are living away from their family. In general, people who feel powerless to improve their situation and lack good support networks undergo great stress, and they may turn the tensions in on themselves and self-harm.

Older self-harmers

It is not only young people who self-harm. Many elderly people face health difficulties, the death of loved ones, and social isolation—large numbers live alone. They experience emotional pain just like young people do and may not have the support to overcome it. Experts believe the suffering of older people may be underestimated because they are unlikely to seek help. They may be better than young people at covering up the evidence and treating the injuries themselves. They may fear that if they talk about it, people will think they have a mental-health condition.

Self-harm in different countries

It appears that self-injury is an international issue, at least in Western cultures.

- In a study of U.S. college students, it was revealed that as many as 32 percent had harmed themselves at least once.
- A 2009 survey compared the percentage of adolescents who self-harmed in U.S. and German schools. There was little statistical difference between the two countries.
- A study on child and adolescent self-harm in Europe investigated the problem in seven European countries. It found that 3 in 10 girls and 1 in 10 boys had either self-harmed or considered doing so in the past year.

Elderly people who live alone may find it hard to cope without emotional support or without help for simple tasks.

What are the warning signs?

A self-harmer may have fresh scars from cuts or cigarette burns, often on the arms or thighs. However, it can be difficult to spot cuts, and bruises can be covered up or excuses can be given. Self-harmers may simply claim they are clumsy and have frequent accidents.

Possible warning signs to look out for include a person covering up in warm weather, even though he or she normally dresses lightly, or avoiding sports that involve showing the body such as swimming. If a person is not doing his or her usual activities, appears withdrawn and lacking in energy, or has unusual mood changes and wants to be alone a lot, these could indicate a problem. Yet there could be other reasons for such behavior, so do not simply assume the person is self-harming.

Mental illness

Most people who self-harm are not mentally ill. However, self-harming may indicate a psychological disorder, such as depression, **bipolar disorder**, or an eating disorder. It could be linked to a **borderline personality disorder (BPD)** (a condition that means the person has great emotional instability and mood swings and acts **impulsively**). People who have a mental illness tend to experience frequent mood changes and distressing thoughts, which put them at increased risk of self-harming.

Eating disorders

Self-harm may be linked to an eating disorder, another behavior concerning control over the body. For some people, self-harming becomes a replacement for the eating disorder. As one woman commented, "When I started to emerge from my **anorexia**, I needed some other way of dealing with the pain and hurt, so I started cutting instead. It is a way of gaining temporary relief."

A self-harmer has described the short-lived relief she experiences in this way: "As the blood flows down the sink, so does the anger and the anguish."

Self-harm and suicidal thoughts in young people

In an international survey, studies of adolescent self-harm and suicidal behavior were compiled, mostly from the United States, and also Europe, Australia, and New Zealand. The survey found that suicidal thoughts are relatively common in adolescents, but a higher proportion of young people engage in self-harm than in suicidal behavior.

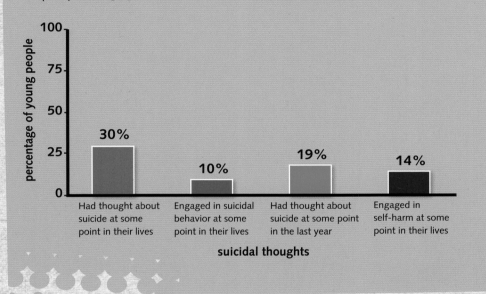

Is self-harm linked to suicide?

Self-harm is very different from suicide. People who attempt suicide want to end their pain and their life completely, while those who self-harm are trying to make themselves feel better and manage the pain. However, a person who self-harms is 50 to 100 times more likely than the general population to later commit suicide. People who self-harm should not be seen as a suicide risk, but they should be helped to address their problems to prevent them from becoming suicidal.

It is important not to be alarmed and to remember that in most young people, self-harm does not signify mental illness or abnormality. It occurs because of distressing or overwhelming episodes and an inability to express emotion in a healthier way. These difficulties can be overcome, as many personal accounts in this book demonstrate.

Survivors of abuse

Some children or young adults may endure **physical**, **emotional**, or sexual abuse or bullying. Children who are neglected or put into foster care have a higher risk of suffering this kind of treatment than others.

If an adult abuses young people, the young people may think that somehow it is their fault. They may therefore feel guilty, and the experience ruins their self-esteem. If they do not have enough support to help them to recover, they might turn the anger inward and resort to harming themselves.

"It expresses emotional pain or feelings that I'm unable to put into words. It puts a punctuation mark on what I'm feeling on the inside!"

A self-harmer explains why she does it

Self-harm may be a way of punishing themselves by reliving the feelings they experienced during their abuse. They may possibly adopt **magical thinking** (the inaccurate belief that a person's thoughts, words, or actions will prevent a specific outcome), believing that if they deliberately injure themselves physically, no greater harm will come to them.

It is hard for people who have been abused to recover from their ordeal. Yet, no matter how long ago the abuse took place and no matter how traumatic the feelings, the problems abuse caused can always be tackled. It is never too late.

TRUE OR FALSE?

People who self-harm have been sexually abused.

False. Many people who self-harm have endured sexual abuse, but this does not mean that everyone who self-harms has been abused.

LILA'S STORY: ABUSE LED ME TO SELF-HARM

"The last few months have been very difficult for me. I was diagnosed with depression and **post-traumatic stress disorder (PTSD)** (mental and emotional problems resulting from a shocking experience). I was struggling in my daily life, fell behind at school, and my friends abandoned me. I wanted to walk away, too, from the mess I was in.

I was distressed because I was abused when I was little. I had never told anyone what had happened and was worried that if I talked about the abuse, it would divide my family and bring back all the buried memories. I started cutting myself as the only way to cope.

It is hard to feel that no one understands what you are going through. Help lines can be an important source of support.

My parents found out about my self-harming, but they simply grew angry with me. When I tried to explain the reason for it, I would break down and have a **panic attack**.

I decided to contact a help line because I didn't know how to stop self-harming. I confided in the help line **counselor**, saying that talking about the abuse was very painful and made me want to die. Cutting was a way of making me feel alive. But what I really wanted to do was to be able to discuss my problems with someone not involved in my life. The help line counselor listened to me carefully and did not push me to reveal any more than I wanted to. The counselor gave me details of a crisis service for girls and women who self-harm, so now I'm going to contact them for help. At least now I know what to do."

HOW DO PEOPLE SELF-HARM?

This young man has many scars from cutting himself.

People self-harm in a variety of ways, from scratching or bruising themselves to serious cutting and burning. The injuries may range from minor wounds to lasting **disfigurement**. Generally, self-harmers do not want others to know about it, so they hurt themselves in private, injuring a part of the body not normally visible to other people. They rarely seek medical help.

What do self-harmers do?

Cutting is the most common form of self-harm, using easily available items such as scissors, razors, or knives. The wound may be superficial (on the surface) or deep, but self-harmers usually try to avoid veins and arteries, because they are not attempting suicide.

Other typical methods are banging or bruising the body—for example, by punching walls or scratching the skin. Some people pull their hair or break their bones. Other people burn themselves with cigarettes or lighters or scald their skin with boiling water.

Eating or drinking drugs or chemicals to cause pain, rather than to end their life, is another way that people self-harm. The most common form of self-harm that results in a hospital visit is overdosing on drugs, usually acetaminophen. Some people swallow toxic substances such as batteries.

Which parts of the body?

Self-harmers tend to injure the arms, hands, stomach, and thighs and less frequently the breasts or sexual organs.

All injuries should be taken seriously, but those working with young people who self-harm say that the more secret and violent the injury, the more concerned they are about the person.

This survey of children and young people shows types of self-harm over a three-month period.

Injury	Percentage
Cutting	25
Inflicting blows	15
Burning/scalding	3
Picking/scratching	20
Pulling out hair	8
Biting	10
Swallowing objects	7
Inserting objects	2
Other	10
Total	**100**

Do self-harmers plan the act?

It seems that most people self-harm impulsively rather than planning the action in advance. The stress builds up, and they cut or burn themselves to release the tension. However, they will usually check to make sure that no one else is around.

"There's often a deep feeling of calm and relief immediately after cutting, although that's rapidly replaced by an overwhelming sense of guilt and revulsion [disgust]."

Mark Smith self-harmed for 13 years after years of bullying and racist abuse. He eventually managed to stop.

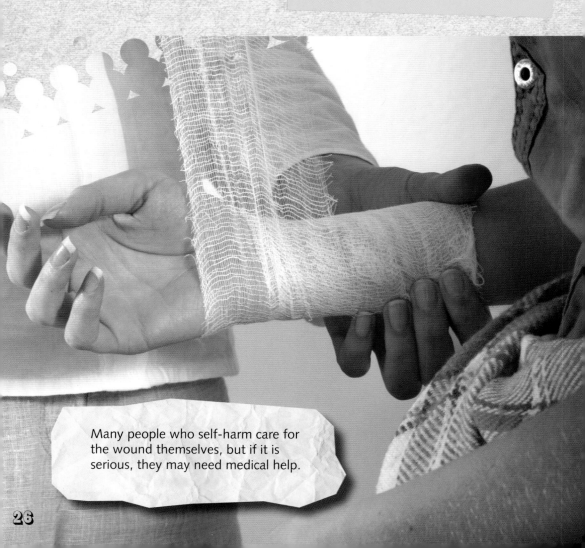

Many people who self-harm care for the wound themselves, but if it is serious, they may need medical help.

How does it make people feel?

At the time it is occurring, self-harm can trigger chemicals in the body called **endorphins**. These chemicals bring on feelings of well-being and relief. During the moment of inflicting the injury, people may not feel pain. Instead, typically, they experience the lack of sensation that occurs during abuse or trauma. The body is numbed and self-harmers feel detached from themselves. However, the pain may come later. In addition, these people may feel guilty and ashamed of their actions; they cover up the wound and hope no one will notice.

For how long and how often?

Some people self-harm on a few occasions during a difficult period and stop when the problems are resolved. For others, self-harming becomes a habit. Some people may hurt themselves once, believing it is a one-time event. They may even self-harm by accident and receive a pleasurable feeling. Then they do it again to achieve the same feeling. However, self-harm is not really about seeking physical pleasure; people use it as a way to cope with their problems or distract themselves from them. Young people may become used to self-harming, and the habit is then born. They may do it regularly—even up to several times a day.

Once people have started self-injuring, it can become hard to kick the habit, even if they want to stop. They might even find they have to inflict an ever-greater amount of harm to achieve the same relief. Their injuries may become increasingly severe and require medical treatment.

Those who experiment with self-harm to fit in with a gang or because of peer pressure may not develop a habit. Regular self-harm usually indicates underlying troubles. No matter how long the self-harming has been going on, even if it is many years, once efforts are made to tackle the issues, it is possible to stop.

THINK ABOUT THIS

Self-harming is just one way to allow people to forget their bad situation for a while. Some people drink alcohol or take drugs to achieve the same effect. What do you think are the similarities and differences between these activities and self-harming?

SEEKING HELP

Confiding in someone is an important first step toward overcoming self-harming behavior.

Many people who self-harm find help and ways to stop. However, it can be hard for people to seek help. Often they feel they can manage on their own. They are concerned about people's reactions and that if they tell someone, their way of coping will be taken away. These fears are genuine, but they can be overcome. Telling someone about self-harming is the first step toward stopping.

Fears at school

Young people are concerned about gossip at school if others find out about their self-harm. This was one girl's experience: "At school my self-harm was treated very badly. It was treated as a piece of gossip by the teachers, and the principal asked me to leave as a result, saying that I was a great person but he couldn't have it in his school."

Some young people are forced to admit to self-harm because teachers or health professionals have guessed that it is happening. Then they become frightened that the professionals will tell others, including their families. Their secret act becomes common knowledge, and they feel they have lost control.

This loss of control is particularly hard to deal with because the self-harming behavior was probably the young person's way of trying to *maintain* control in a difficult situation. Furthermore, once others know about what is going on, they are likely to monitor the person to check if he or she is self-harming, focusing on the action itself rather than helping to address the root of the problem.

Who to tell?

Not knowing who to contact can be a problem. If self-harmers had been comfortable with talking to someone else about their troubles, perhaps they would not have felt the need to self-harm in the first place. They may be anxious about what other people will think of them or fear a lack of understanding. Girls tend to worry that people will think they are seeking attention, while boys frequently feel their injuries and situation are not serious enough to require intervention.

Fear of being shunned

Young people may be afraid that if they become known as self-harmers, others might view them as mentally ill, and they might lose their friends. They are also concerned that it could affect their work opportunities in the future—that they could be seen as "dangerous" or "sick" and not allowed to work in teaching, nursing, or childcare. However, these fears are unfounded. Many people self-harm for a period but then solve their problems, continue with their education, and enter working life like everyone else.

THINK ABOUT THIS

People go to the hospital for many reasons, including accidents, alcohol- or smoking-related diseases, and self-harm. Do they all deserve equal care?

The experts in an emergency room are usually extremely busy and often stressed. Some of them may not be very sympathetic to self-harmers.

Reactions from health workers

Nevertheless, young people have understandable concerns about contacting health professionals about self-harming. Not all health professionals are sympathetic. In hospital emergency rooms, doctors and nurses are sometimes rude to self-harmers because they believe they are time-wasters or that they are merely seeking attention. A former director of nursing explained this attitude: "Often, emergency room nurses and doctors react negatively because they're stressed out dealing with many serious injuries, from a grandmother who's been beaten up to a child burned in a house fire, so someone who's cut themselves may not be regarded as deserving the same priority." In such circumstances, would you find it easy to be understanding?

Some young people have found their experience of asking for help has made things worse, because the professionals they hoped would help them have been hostile. It makes them decide not to talk about what is happening to them. On the other hand, some young people have met with acceptance by hospital workers who have not judged their actions but rather have treated them sympathetically and dealt with their wounds. Therefore, young people should not be discouraged from seeking help if they have a bad experience, but rather should try to be patient and approach someone else.

When people use emergency services, they urgently require medical attention. However, the deep-rooted causes of the self-harm remain, so they need to be offered further help.

Two experiences of hospital services

"My treatment from people in emergency rooms varied from indifferent to downright vicious and humiliating. This ranged from doctors telling me I was wasting bed space, to having butterfly strips [suitable only for shallow wounds] put on—instead of stitches—and being kept waiting for hours."

Former self-harmer Mark Smith

"He ... took great pains to suture [sew up the wound] very neatly. When I commented on this he said, 'I don't want it to leave any scars,' to which I replied that I am covered in them. He said 'not on my watch.'"

A self-harmer reports a positive experience in the hospital

Who can help?

At first, many people prefer to talk about their self-harm to a friend, family member, or trusted adult in their school. Professionals such as a doctor, nurse, or youth counselor are good people to contact, too. For those who are not ready to talk face-to-face, an online or telephone help line is useful, allowing the person to remain **anonymous**.

Friend or professional?

If an individual opts to talk to a friend or family member about self-harming, it will probably be hard for the listener, too. The friend or relative is emotionally involved with the person and may be upset, express shock, or find the behavior extremely hard to understand. A professional, such as a doctor or counselor, will be detached enough to listen without alarm and will not be hurt by the details.

TRUE OR FALSE?

It is easy to stop self-harming.

Generally false. People can usually only stop self-harming by working through the feelings that led to it in the first place. This can be hard, but ultimately rewarding, work.

These young people are discussing their problems in a group therapy session.

Preparing to talk about self-harm

- Consider where and when you would tell the person.
- Decide how to have the conversation. Would you feel more comfortable talking face-to-face, on the phone, or online?
- Figure out what to say, perhaps by making some notes. See if you can explain the feelings that lead you to self-harm, rather than focusing on the actual injuries.
- Think about what you want from the other person. Do you want someone to just listen or to offer some advice?
- Be prepared for disappointment! The first person you speak to might not be able to help, and you may need to find someone else.

Professionals who can help

Once the topic is out in the open, it may be enough to simply find the right person to talk to and discuss how to sort out the issues. A variety of professionals can also offer assistance. Family doctors can recommend social workers, specialists, and counselors. Various kinds of **therapy** and counseling are available.

One is **cognitive behavioral therapy (CBT)**. This practical therapy helps people to talk about how they think about themselves and others and how what they do affects their thoughts and feelings. A CBT therapist can help a person to look at the triggers for self-harm and encourage the person to find other ways to express his or her emotions.

In some cases, a doctor may prescribe medication (drugs), such as **antidepressants**. These drugs can help to treat underlying depression and anxiety.

Some people find **self-help groups** useful. These enable people with similar dilemmas to offer each other practical advice and support. Another option is **group therapy**, where a trained therapist works with a group of people who have self-harmed. They realize that they are not alone and share their problems. There are so many kinds of treatments available that there is bound to be something to suit everyone.

HOW TO HELP A FRIEND OR RELATIVE

Self-harmers often keep their difficulties to themselves. However, it can be really helpful to share problems with a trusted friend.

If someone you know tells you that he or she is self-harming, the person has acted courageously by admitting it. The reaction the person receives affects what happens next. The person needs the chance to talk about the feelings that led to the self-harming. A calm response will help the self-harmer to seek assistance and recover.

Don't panic!

It is important to keep an open mind and try not to sound shocked. The person has chosen you to listen, so hear what he or she has to say without judgment or condemnation. You may be disgusted by it, but keep this to yourself. As one former self-harmer says, "Self-harmers feel enough shame without people adding to it." Let the self-harmer take the discussion at his or her own pace and do not push the person to say more than he or she is comfortable to reveal.

If the person is scared about injuring himself or herself more than was intended, encourage the self-harmer to attend to the wounds before discussing any troubles. A friend who is trained in basic first aid may be able to help. If in doubt, however, always call 911.

Keeping self-harm secret?

The self-harmer may ask you not to tell anyone about the self-harming. This puts you in a difficult position, especially if are you unsure how much danger the person is in. Think carefully: Do you know an older person you can confide in and trust to keep the matter secret? Try to find the right person to offer you advice and help you figure out what to do.

TRUE OR FALSE?

Even if the wound is not a major one, the problem causing the self-harm is serious.

True. Self-harming should always be taken seriously, no matter the size of the wound.

Offering reassurance and support

Try to reassure the person that you still care about him or her no matter what the person is going through, and that you will offer support, even if you cannot understand exactly why the person is self-harming. Allow the self-harmer to talk freely. Do not tell him or her to stop self-harming or place conditions on behavior, such as punishment if the person continues to do it. There is no point in taking away the tools the person uses for self-harm; he or she will simply find something else. If you react in this way, the person may not want to talk to you about the self-harm anymore, and an opportunity to resolve the problems could be lost. The decision to stop has to come from the self-harmer.

Try not to take it personally if the person is close to you. People do not injure themselves to make a point to others around them; it is about how they are feeling inside. The person is telling you because he or she trusts you and believes you can offer support. Acknowledge that the person is in pain and encourage him or her to believe that the situation can improve in time.

It may be that all the person needs is someone to listen. But you may feel unable to help the person. You could suggest that the self-harmer share his or her feelings with others who might be able to assist or help find a doctor. There may be underlying issues such as anxiety and depression that a doctor could diagnose. However, do not tell the person what to do, or he or she may feel the situation is out of control. Remember that self-harming may be the only way the person feels he or she can exercise some control over life at this time. If the self-harmer does decide to see a doctor, you could offer to go along for support.

TRUE OR FALSE?

Self-harmers are attention seekers.

False. They usually want to hide their actions and only seek medical attention if the injury has gone too far. They are trying to cope with pain or pressure; what they really seek is care.

A good friend listens without judgment.

Take care of yourself

Find out more about self-harm through books and web sites so you understand it better and can be more supportive. This will also help you to deal with your own feelings. It is difficult to accept that someone close to you is self-harming. It may make you feel hurt, angry, or powerless, and you might need some counseling or other assistance yourself. To find out more, see the research advice on pages 50–51.

"Young people want quotes or advice from people who have suffered from self-harm (especially people who have beaten it) for encouragement, because it makes the advice more valid to know they've experienced it all and know what they're talking about."

The view of a young self-harmer

SAMIRA'S STORY: A FRIEND HELPED ME TO STOP SELF-HARMING

"When I look back, I can see that I couldn't handle trying to be someone I wasn't. I was crying out for help, but no one could hear me—neither friends nor family. It was like I had a little girl in my heart, screaming out desperately for help, and no one was there.

It all started in school. There was so much pressure on me to do well, both from my family and the school. But I knew I couldn't do it, I just wasn't the academic type. My science classes were hell. I was put with people I really hated. There was just one person I could talk to, a tutor who helped me after class. It was good to have a shoulder to cry on, and after difficult classes I took time out to speak to this person.

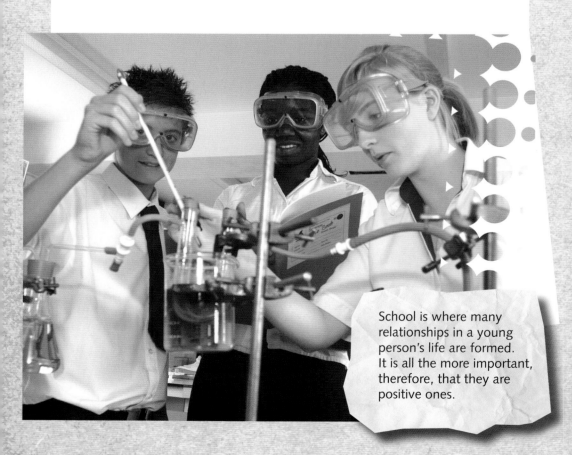

School is where many relationships in a young person's life are formed. It is all the more important, therefore, that they are positive ones.

When it was time for my exams I panicked. I felt that I was stupid and a disappointment to everyone. I was such a failure! That day, I went home and took the scissors from my mom's desk. I hid in the corner of my room with the door shut and started to cut my wrists. I didn't have any feelings about what I'd done until the next morning, when the pain kicked in. The wounds didn't show when I was wearing my school uniform. I hadn't really thought about whether anyone at home would notice.

Every day after school, I made sure no one else was upstairs, and I took the scissors and cut myself. This continued for a couple of years. The day when I found out a good friend was self-harming as well was the day I knew this behavior had to stop.

I went every day to see the tutor. By now, we had become friends. Spending time with a trusted friend was an important part of the process of weaning myself off the self-harming. The year flew by. I'm a bit older now and although I have cut myself since then, I haven't ever cut myself as much or as badly as I did before. Now I have my own counselor, who is amazing, and I have good friends to talk to. I never told my parents, but they're not stupid, so I guess they know. But they still love and support me. They are my rock."

TRUE OR FALSE?

A person who has been self-harming for years cannot be helped.

False. Everyone can be helped, with the right support.

HOW TO STOP SELF-HARMING

Going for a run is a simple and effective way to reduce stress.

To stop self-harming, the first step is to accept that the harm is occurring and find someone to talk to. It is also good to adopt distraction techniques and figure out how to reduce the impulse to self-harm.

People who have self-harmed report a variety of emotions that provoked the decision to seek help to stop. Sometimes they feel angry or hate themselves—they are scared they might cause lasting damage, but feel powerless to stop. They may sense that the self-harm has gotten out of control and worry about what others might think if they find out. It brings feelings of guilt and shame.

To help themselves, people can try to interpret their own behavior. What was happening when they started to self-harm? Was it a particular event, or do they experience frightening memories or thoughts? It is usually possible to figure out what triggers the self-harming.

Improving coping strategies

People can also consider how to improve their coping strategies in general, so that when stress arises, they can find an outlet for their emotions. Often just talking to a friend or contacting a help line can be enough. Some people find it useful to keep a diary of their feelings or to take up a form of exercise. Keeping away from tools used for self-harm can reduce the temptation.

Developing an awareness of the body is worthwhile, too. The body and mind are closely linked, and people frequently express their feelings through their body—they may find it hard to sleep or have panic attacks, or they may self-harm. If people learn to cope better, they are less likely to inflict pain on their own body.

"I tried so many [options]—I found it hard to adapt to something different, when I was used to coping with my own way. Eventually, though, I found a way of coping that I moved forward with, and it helped me to stop."

Young self-harmer

Self-harm minimization

The **self-harm minimization** approach has been adopted by professionals in the United States and internationally to help self-harmers tackle their difficulties. The principle is similar to approaches taken with drug or alcohol users. If people are forbidden to self-harm or are punished for doing so, it is likely to drive the behavior underground and will not solve the underlying issues. This approach can be defined as "accepting the need to self-harm as a valid method of survival until survival is possible by other means." It does not encourage self-injury, but rather accepts that if self-harm is going to take place, it is better to do it as safely as possible. With self-harm minimization, people who are not yet ready or able to stop self-harming can learn to alter their behavior to lessen the impact. For example, they can avoid cutting risky areas, such as the wrists, which contain arteries, and instead cut a more fleshy part of the body. Although harm minimization recognizes that self-injury will still happen, self-harmers are offered other forms of support, such as counseling, to improve their coping strategies and try to tackle the cause of distress.

One method of self-harm minimization is to cool a burned area under running water for at least 15 minutes.

Emergency situations

If you find someone who is experiencing serious bleeding or burns, call 911 immediately and find an adult to help. If the person has taken poison, put the person in the recovery position, if you know how to do this. Do not make the person vomit unless a health professional tells you to.

ACKNOWLEDGING THE PROBLEM: DEPRESSION

Tamsin, 13, had been bullied by a boy for two years. In all that time, she told no one. Eventually she told her best friend, who convinced her to tell an adult. She spoke to her Scout leader, and the bullying was stopped.

But this was not the end of it. Tamsin had started to believe what the bully had told her—that she was fat and ugly. She became really depressed and after three months, just after her fourteenth birthday, she started cutting herself. Tamsin did not cut deep enough to cause damage, so her parents did not notice.

But Tamsin knew she had a problem, and even in the depths of her misery she realized she needed to do something about it. She talked to her Scout leader again, who persuaded her to see her family doctor. It took a lot of courage to visit him. The doctor told Tamsin he thought she was depressed, but instead of prescribing drugs, he wrote to her school nurse. Tamsin went to speak with her regularly, and she managed to stop cutting herself. Gradually, she became happier again, and eventually she felt able to tell her parents what had happened. Tamsin says, "My advice to anyone reading this is to tell someone because even if it does seem scary and nerve-wracking it will help in the long run. It's always nice to have someone to listen to your problems."

Distraction

Many people who self-harm discover distraction techniques. When they feel the urge to hurt themselves, they focus on an activity that works for them until the desire has gone. It can be an activity as simple as listening to music, watching television, or going outdoors. Some people find that writing soothes them. They may write a diary of their feelings and emotions, assess the pros and cons of self-harming, or describe what is making them angry or upset. People may write positive statements about themselves to build their self-esteem or focus on happy events, such as vacations. Talking to others often helps, too. Many people find it is handy to keep the numbers of friends or help lines close at all times, so they can call if they need to. Others employ the five minutes rule (see the box below).

Outlets for feelings

Some people find harmless outlets for their anger, such as beating pillows or cushions. They go somewhere they will not disturb anyone and shout and scream as loud as they can to release tension. Substitute behaviors—that is, alternatives to self-harm—work for some people. They might use a red pen to mark the skin instead of cutting it or put red food coloring in ice cubes and melt them in the hand to resemble blood. Others rub themselves with ice. Another technique is to flick rubber bands on the wrist. All of these activities provide release, but they cause no damage.

"I tried holding an ice-cube, rubber band flicking on the wrist, writing down my thoughts, hitting a pillow, listening to music, writing down pros and cons-but the most helpful to my recovery was the five minutes rule, where if you feel like you want to self-harm you wait for five minutes before you do it, then see if you can go another five minutes, and so on, till eventually the urge is over."

A young person describes how he began to tackle self-harming

> "I cut because I needed to see blood, so I painted my nails red and dyed my hair red so I could see the color flow down the sink."

Kirsti Reeve found therapy useful but also practiced substitute behavior

A creative activity, such as playing a musical instrument, can be good for expressing your feelings as well as for relieving tension.

Stress relievers

In general, it is worth searching for ways to make life less stressful. If people take care of their health by eating regularly and exercising, they generally feel happier. Just going for a walk in the park can be restful. Regularly practicing relaxation techniques such as yoga, meditation, or deep-breathing exercises helps to reduce tension. Creative activities such as art or music are a great way to express feelings. You do not need to be a musician. Even singing in the shower can be extremely therapeutic!

Reducing the impulse

People often need to try different options for reducing self-harm until they find something that works for them. It is important to be patient. Usually, once people have the opportunity to talk about the underlying feelings that have overwhelmed them, the impulse to self-harm is reduced. Self-harm is a form of communication—a means of expressing pain without talking about it. If the problem is brought out into the open and is no longer kept secret, then people will feel less need to self-harm. They are communicating their difficulties in words instead. It may still take time to change the circumstances that led people to self-harm, but discussing troubles is the important first step.

"I belong to a women's self-harm support group. The group was the start of changing my life. The encouragement and support has given me the strength and courage to continue my life, and I now value myself. I still self-harm, but nowhere near as much as I used to. By talking about it, I am learning to deal with my feelings."

Recovering self-harmer

"I feel a lot more confident. I've learned to be more open about my feelings and been able to move on . . . I've been able to come out of myself and explain what I do, and make sense of it, not keep having to lie and cover up what I did. I no longer feel ashamed since I know people are supporting me."

Former self-harmer

HANNAH'S STORY:
I FOUND ALTERNATIVES TO SELF-HARM

"I began self-harming when I was 14. I was feeling stressed out because my parents were splitting up. They were having their own difficulties, so I didn't want to burden them with my problems. But the situation just grew worse and worse. I realize now that I should have talked to my parents or friends before going down the road of self-harm. At the time, though, I couldn't see a way out.

One day I had a huge argument with my mom and I went and hurt myself. I found that it relieved the pressure that had built up inside me. So then every time I felt angry or stressed, I would self-harm. Each time I told myself this would be the last time. But then I hurt myself so badly that I had to go to the hospital, and I got the courage to tell my parents. It was hard to talk about it, but it was the first step to getting better. They felt upset but helped me.

I began to see a counselor, who encouraged me to seek ways to de-stress without self-harming. I discovered that I loved writing poems and stories, so when I felt like hurting myself, I started writing instead. Finding other things to do took my mind off self-harming, and I began to do it less often. Now I haven't self-harmed for over 18 months. I feel stronger because I have found a way to cope when things get tough."

Writing poetry or stories and keeping a diary are good ways to find an outlet for confusing emotions.

WHAT CAN BE DONE TO ADDRESS SELF-HARM?

Young people who self-harm need support and assistance to address the underlying reasons that cause the behavior. Educating families, peer groups, and all the people who work with young people can increase understanding of self-harm.

"We're expected to be good daughters/sons, good siblings, very good students, thin and beautiful, talented, and good friends. Constantly these expectations are far too high for teenagers to meet, and so we come to think it's our own fault, and gradually, begin to hate ourselves for not being able to meet society's expectations."

A former self-harmer reflects on the pressures on young people

The role of families

It is essential for parents to listen to their children's concerns. Even if a problem may appear minor to the adult, it could be very important to the young person. Parents should be supportive, always give plenty of praise for positive behavior, and help their children to set reasonable goals. Families need guidance on how to cope if a child turns to self-harm and reveals it to them.

How schools can help

School-wide measures, such as anti-bullying programs, have been shown to be effective. This proves that everyone can have troubles, and that this is completely normal. Through programs like this, people will realize they are not alone.

Teachers and administrators need to provide opportunities for students to discuss issues, rather than expecting them to come forward to talk. They should also accept that self-harm is going on. Providing information to young people should be a top priority, since those who self-harm are most likely to turn to friends for support. It is also useful to set up safe channels of communication for students to report difficulties at school. This all helps to reduce the **stigma** often attached to self-harm and makes it simpler for young people to seek assistance.

Peer support groups can be set up to allow students to help each other out with problems. The groups can tackle topics such as coping with exams and building self-esteem. It is not only students who need to be educated, however. Awareness of self-harm should be raised among the adults working in the school as well. They need to understand it better so they can deal with it rationally and calmly and learn to advise their students about support services.

Investing in young people

All health professionals and other adults working with young people should be well-informed on the subject, too. If money is invested in local support services, young self-harmers can begin to learn how to sort out their difficulties and get on with their lives.

This student is helping to paint an anti-bullying mural at her school. Everyone can get involved in helping each other overcome their specific problems.

RESEARCH AND DEBATE

You can find out more about self-harm from a variety of sources. Think about whether your source is reliable and consider the perspective of the person who produced it. Might the person be trying to promote a particular point of view?

Books

Nonfiction books written for young people are an excellent source of accurate and accessible information. Written by professional writers and checked by experts, the materials have been designed especially for young readers and provide a balanced view of the topic, backed up by evidence. Check the publication date of the book and try to find the most up-to-date titles.

Web sites

Web sites run by highly respected, established organizations working with people who self-harm, such as mental-health organizations, are excellent sources of trustworthy information (see pages 54–55). They usually have case studies and quotes from people who have self-harmed, so you can find firsthand information about other people's experiences.

Firsthand information is also available from surveys about self-harm. Organizations working with young people often publish the results of their research online. Check that the source is recent to ensure the information is up-to-date.

A warning about sources

Not all web sites are helpful or reliable. Anyone can set up a web site or blog and write what they like; no one checks if it is true or not. Beware of sites that are run by individuals and express their point of view alone.

There are self-harm web sites on which people who self-injure publicize their activities, often through images and videos. Some young people use self-harm web sites to get their voice heard and discuss issues with others in the same situation. But all information on such sites should be considered the opinion of the writer alone.

Organize your research materials

If you are researching self-harm for a school project, start by organizing your research materials into different categories. You could use the concept web below as a starting point:

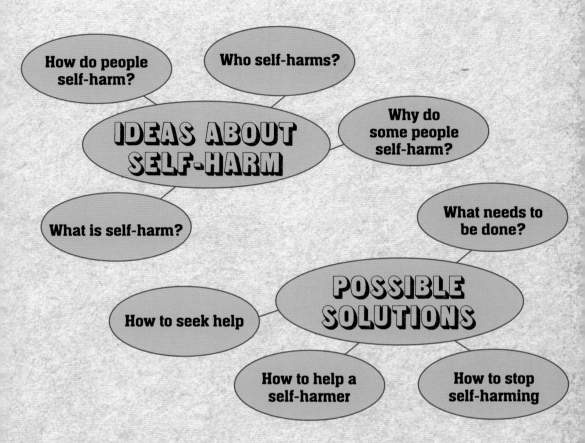

Using information for discussion and debate

If you are planning a discussion about self-harm, remember that it is an extremely sensitive topic. Remember that in a class of 30 students, on average there will be about two who have self-harmed, although others may not know about it. You may want to use role-playing in your debate. Different groups could adopt a different perspective on self-harm and argue from that point of view. You could use the topics in the "Think about this" boxes in this book as discussion points.

GLOSSARY

abuse cruel or violent treatment of people; to use wrongly

anonymous when someone communicates without giving his or her name

anorexia disorder in which the person has an abnormal fear of being overweight, leading to dangerous weight loss

antidepressant drug used to treat depression

bipolar disorder disorder in which the person has dramatic mood swings, from extreme happiness to intense despair

borderline personality disorder (BPD) serious mental illness that causes huge mood swings, self-image problems, impulsive behavior, and difficulties in maintaining relationships with other people

clique small group of people who spend their time together and do not allow others to join them

cognitive behavioral therapy (CBT) talking therapy that helps people to change how they think (cognitive) and what they do (behavior)

counselor person who has been trained to advise people with problems, especially personal problems

depression medical condition that makes a person feel very sad and anxious

discrimination treating a particular group in society unfairly—for example, because of their race, religion, or gender

disfigurement ruin or alter the appearance of

distraction something that takes your attention away from what you are doing or thinking about

eating disorder having an abnormal attitude toward food that causes a person to change his or her eating habits—for example, trying to keep one's weight as low as possible, or overeating by bingeing on food

emotional abuse using words or gestures to gain power and control over another person—for example, acting aggressively toward people or neglecting them

empathy ability to understand another person's feelings

endorphin hormone released in the brain and nervous system that can cause feelings of well-being

euphoric describes a strong feeling of happiness that usually lasts only a short time

group therapy when a group of people meets to discuss a shared problem, with a trained group therapist to guide and support them

impulsive doing something without thinking

magical thinking inaccurate belief that a person's thoughts, words, or actions will prevent a specific outcome

panic attack exaggeration of the body's normal reaction to fear, which can cause very rapid breathing, dizziness, sweating, and/or feelings of terror

peer person who is the same age and in the same social circle as you

physical abuse when someone physically injures a person—for example, by hitting or kicking the person

post-traumatic stress disorder (PTSD) mental and emotional problems resulting from a shocking experience

psychological relating to a person's mind

self-destructive damaging to oneself

self-esteem feeling of being happy with your own character and abilities

self-harm minimization reducing the harm caused by self-injury—for example, by keeping wounds clean

self-help group group of people who work together to reach a shared goal—for example, to help each other to overcome a problem

sexual abuse when a child or young person is forced to take part in any kind of sexual activity with an adult or young person

stigma feelings of disapproval that people have about particular illnesses or ways of behaving

suicide act of killing yourself on purpose

symptom sign that something exists, especially a problem

therapy treatment of an illness or physical problem

traumatic extremely unpleasant and causing great distress

trigger something that causes a particular action, especially a bad one

vulnerable easily hurt, either physically or emotionally

FIND OUT MORE

Books

Nonfiction

Allman, Toney. *Self-Injury* (Hot Topics). Detroit: Lucent, 2011.

Barnett Veague, Heather. *Cutting and Self-Harm* (Psychological Disorders). New York: Chelsea House, 2008.

Eagen, Rachel. *Cutting and Self-Injury* (Straight Talk About...). New York: Crabtree, 2011.

Esherick, Joan. *The Silent Cry: A Teen's Guide to Escaping Self-Injury and Suicide* (Science of Health). Philadelphia: Mason Crest, 2005.

Hile, Lori. *Bullying* (Teen Issues). Chicago: Heinemann Library, 2013.

Powell, Jillian. *Self-Harm and Suicide* (Emotional Health Issues). Pleasantville, N.Y.: Gareth Stevens, 2009.

Shapiro, Lawrence E. *Stopping the Pain: A Workbook for Teens Who Cut and Self-Injure*. Oakland, Calif.: Instant Help, 2008.

Williams, Mary E. *Self-Mutilation* (Introducing Issues with Opposing Viewpoints). Detroit: Greenhaven, 2009.

Fiction

Dzidrums, Christine. *Cutters Don't Cry*. Whittier, Calif.: Creative Media, 2010.

Web sites

www.girlshealth.gov/feelings/sad/cutting.cfm
This government web site discusses girls and self-harm, as well as a variety of other issues affecting young women.

www.helpguide.org/mental/self_injury.htm
Find cutting and self-injury support on this web site, including links to useful resources.

kidshealth.org/teen/your_mind/feeling_sad/cutting.html
This web site offers more information about teens and cutting.

www.recoveryourlife.com
Recover Your Life is an organization that specializes in dealing with self-harm. Visit this web site to find forums, advice, and more.

www.safe-alternatives.com
S.A.F.E. Alternatives is an organization that offers treatment and advice for people dealing with self-harm.

www.stopbullying.gov
This government web site offers resources on bullying for kids, teens, parents, and educators.

www.teenhealthandwellness.com/static/hotlines
Use this web site to find help lines that are specific to a variety of issues mentioned in this book.

teenlineonline.org
If you are facing difficult issues in your life, you might want to talk to someone privately. Visit Teen Line online or call 800-852-8336. You can tell their advisors what is happening to you and they will give you help and advice. You can also look on the message boards to talk to other young people, so you will not feel so alone.

teens.webmd.com/cutting-self-injury
This web site explores the issue of cutting.

www.youngwomenshealth.org/si.html
This web site is aimed at girls and includes more information about self-harming.

Topics to debate

- Do you think showing self-harm on television programs and discussing it in schools encourages the practice? Or does it help sufferers to feel more confident about coming forward?

- What are some of the pressures that society places on young people? Do you think there is a way to lessen these expectations, or are they simply a normal part of growing up?

- Do you think the adults in your life are aware of the problem of self-harm among young people? Are there any things you and your friends could do to raise awareness about the issue in your school?

INDEX